An I Can Read Book®

CHESTER

Story and pictures by SYD HOFF

HarperCollins*Publishers*

CHESTER
Copyright © 1961 by Syd Hoff
Copyright renewed 1989 by Syd Hoff

Library of Congress Catalog Card Number: 61-5768
ISBN 0-06-022455-X
ISBN 0-06-022456-8 (lib. bdg.)
ISBN 0-06-444095-8 (pbk.)

17 18 SCP 30 29

Chester was a wild horse.

He lived out West

with other wild horses.

"I wish someone loved me,"

said Chester.

"I wish someone took care of me."

"You are silly,"

said the other horses.

"It is fun to be wild."

One day men came with ropes.

They were looking for wild horses.

"I am glad to see you,"

said Chester.

"Please put a rope on me."

7

"That horse cannot run,"

said the men.

"We do not want him."

They took all the other horses.

They did not take Chester.

"No one wants me either,"

said a skunk.

"I think I know why,"

said Chester.

He left in a hurry.

11

Chester ran and ran.

He came to a farm.

"Maybe someone here wants me,"

he said.

"You can't give milk,"

said a cow.

"You can't lay eggs,"
said a hen.

"And I pull the wagon around here,"
said a white horse.

"Good-by," said Chester.

He walked down the road.

A car came by.

"This car has 250 horse power,"

said the man in the car.

"I have one horse power,"

said Chester.

18

The car stopped at a gas station.

Chester stopped too.

"I'll have ten gallons of gas,"
said the man.

"I'll have ten gallons of water,"
said Chester.

Chester saw a sign.

"I am hungry," he said.

21

"Oh, dear, I did not
see the first letter.
I cannot eat 'COATS,'"
said Chester.

22

Chester saw a fruit store.

"I'll have a pound of apples,"

said a lady.

"I'll have a pound too,"

said Chester.

"Can you pay for them?"

said the man.

"No," said Chester.

"Then come back when you can pay," said the man.

"All right," said Chester.

"Your apples are good."

25

Chester looked in a house.

A lady was having tea.

"How much sugar do you want?"

she said.

"As much as I can have,"

said Chester.

Chester went by a toy store.

"I wish I had a rocking horse,"

said a child.

"I can be a rocking horse,"
said Chester. "Look!"

"You are too big for our house,"
said the mother.

Chester saw a statue of a horse.

"Maybe I can be a statue," he said.

He stood very still.

All the people thought he was a statue.

All the birds thought he was a statue.

Chester saw a lady

with a feather in her hat.

35

"I will sneeze

if that feather touches my nose,"

said Chester.

The feather touched his nose.

"AH-CHOO!"

38

"Statues don't sneeze,"

said the birds and the people.

"Horses do," said Chester.

He walked away.

Chester walked by a fire house.

"Long ago horses pulled the fire engines,"
said a man.

The bells rang!

There was a fire some place.

Down the poles came the firemen.

They could not start the engine.

"What will we do?"

said the firemen.

"I will get you there in time,"

said Chester.

Down the street they went.

"Clang! Clang! Clang!"

said Chester.

He got them there in time.

"Thank you," said the firemen.

"The engine is running again.

We do not need you now."

Chester walked and walked.

He saw a merry-go-round.

"I think they need me here,"
he said.

The children ran to the horses.

One little boy got on Chester.

Around and around they went!

The children loved the ride.

So did Chester.

The ride ended.

The children got off the horses.

"My horse was real,"

said the little boy.

"He was not real,"

said the children.

"Merry-go-round horses

are never real."

"A real horse runs

when you say 'Giddyap!'"

said one child.

"Let's say it,"

said another child.

They all said it together.

"GIDDYAP!"

Chester ran.

He ran and ran and ran.

The men with ropes saw him.

"Whoa!" they said.

"Do you still want to come with us?"
said the men.

"Yes," said Chester.

They took him to a bright, clean stable.

All the other horses were there.

"You were right, Chester,"
said the horses.
"It is fun here.
It is nice to be loved
and cared for."

"That makes sense," said Chester.

"Good horse sense."